JAKE M

GRAPHIC

KEEPING FOOTBALL IN THE FAMILY

STONE ARCH BOOKS
a capstone imprint

JAKE MADDOX
GRAPHIC NOVELS

Published by Stone Arch Books,
an imprint of Capstone.
1710 Roe Crest Drive
North Mankato, Minnesota 56003
capstonepub.com

Library of Congress Cataloging-in-Publication Data
Names: Maddox, Jake, author. | Muñiz, Berenice, illustrator.
Title: Keeping football in the family / Jake Maddox ; illustrated by Berenice Muñiz.
Description: North Mankato, Minnesota : Stone Arch Books, 2023. | Series: Jake Maddox graphic novels | Audience: Ages 8-12 | Audience: Grades 4-6 | Summary: Alejandro is having trouble living up to his brother's reputation as a great high school quarterback, but his sister Izzy just might be the secret weapon he needs.
Identifiers: LCCN 2022029394 (print) | LCCN 2022029395 (ebook) | ISBN 9781666341188 (hardcover) | ISBN 9781666341225 (paperback) | ISBN 9781666341232 (pdf) | ISBN 9781666341256 (kindle edition)
Subjects: CYAC: Graphic novels. | Football—Fiction. | Brothers and sisters—Fiction. | LCGFT: Sports comics. | Graphic novels.
Classification: LCC PZ7.7.M332 Ke 2023 (print) | LCC PZ7.7.M332 (ebook) | DDC 741.5/973—dc23/eng/20220815
LC record available at https://lccn.loc.gov/2022029394
LC ebook record available at https://lccn.loc.gov/2022029395

Editor: Mandy Robbins
Designer: Heidi Thompson
Production Specialist: Tori Abraham

Printed and bound in the USA. PO5195

KEEPING FOOTBALL IN THE FAMILY

Text by Daniel Mauleón

Art by Berenice Muñiz

Color by Amaury Maldonado

CAST OF CHARACTERS

Eddy

Coach J.

Head Coach Vince

Last year . . .
Last fall, I watched from the sidelines as my older brother Eduardo played his last game of football. It was the state championship, and he had time for one last pass. We were down 21-17. We needed a touchdown.
Eddy was the first of the family to play football. He fell in love with the sport. When he needed someone to practice with, he picked me. He even taught my sister strategy through football video games.

Eddy didn't just enjoy football. He was good. He was captain and quarterback of our high school team. He even worked with the coaches to design the plays.
So when he said he wouldn't play in college, everyone was shocked.
College ball was too demanding, and he wanted to focus on studying.
I swear the field went silent when he made his final throw.

TOUCHDOWN!
The team stormed the field. The crowd cheered. But not Eddy . . .
Eddy turned and pretended to pass me the ball. He ended his imaginary pass pointing at me.
I think it was his way of telling me it's my turn to carry on his football legacy.

This year.
HOME
AWAY
13
So far, I'm doing
a terrible job.

Our record for the season is two wins and two losses. And they were lucky wins. If we want any chance at the playoffs, we need to start racking up wins.
Hut—
Hut—
No matter how hard I try to focus during the game, I feel the pressure to be as great as Eddy. It's like his shadow looms over me all the time.
Just one good pass and we can score a touchdown to win the game.

Just . . .

. . . one . . .

. . . good . . .

OOF!

After the game—and coach telling me to get it together—I tried to catch up on homework.

My brother, the star quarterback of Phillip's High—

Then in came Isabela, or Izzy. She's my older sister.

Oh, it's you Alejandro?! Sorry, I must have confused you for Eddy.

She can be a real twerp sometimes.

I saw your game tonight. You know you have to actually *pass* the ball to win, right?

I knew she was just teasing me, but I wasn't in the mood to play along.

Not now, Iz. Don't you think I feel bad enough?
I—I'm sorry. I went too far.
That was a tough loss.

But maybe I can help.

Pfft! How could *you* help?

I've been watching all season, and I have some ideas. You've never been a quick thinker like me or Eddy.

Hey!
Sorry! What I'm trying to say is you need plays to help you make better decisions in the moment. Here—
—it will be easier—
—if I just—
—show you.

Like Eddy, your plays focus on passing. But you keep bunching up your offensive line.
You don't give your receivers a chance to break away. You need to give them clearer paths, so they don't run into each other or the other team. This is something Eddy understood.
30
40
50
HB
huff
And *you* understand this too?

Just because you spend all day hiding in the basement playing video games, doesn't make you quarterback material.

You know what? Fine.

I was just trying to help.
Well I don't need it.

thwak

As much as I hated it, Izzy was right. Eddy was the perfect quarterback. He was decisive, smart, a great leader. Sure, I might have a stronger throwing arm. But that doesn't help if I can't direct my team where to go.

Still, I didn't need *her* help.

At practice that week, our assistant coach, Coach J., called me over. He had taken over a lot of the team responsibilities while our head coach was focusing on health issues.

We need to have a serious chat.

What's up Coach?

Alejandro, you need to shape up. I've given you a lot of chances this season—five games' worth.
If you can't figure out how to throw a clean pass, I'm going to have to bench you.

I've got a winning playbook—the same ones Coach Vince and your brother built together. But they don't seem to be working for you. So, tell me—

—do *you* have any of that family genius?
Coach was right. I wasn't playing like Eddy . . .

Wait, Coach! I have a new play I want to try at today's practice.

I took the offensive line through Izzy's play.

I've got a new play, which will give us more options. So far we've been bunching you all up too much. This play should give you a chance to break away.

I took a deep breath then . . .

Hut— hut!

I watch as my team spreads out the defense.

TOUCHDOWN!
21
16
8
13
Now *that's* a great play! Did Eddy help you? Or was that all you?
What can I say? I've got a few good ideas.
Well keep them coming!
I considered telling Coach J. that it was Izzy's play, but I really needed a win.

If I wanted more plays, I needed to go to Izzy. But I was worried she would still be mad at me.

Umm . . . I wanted to say sorry for the other night, and . . . you're play worked really well in practice.

Really? You tried it? And it worked? I mean, of *course* it did.
Yeah, it was great. I actually came down to ask if you had more.

Are you still mad?
What? Oh no, I forgive you. Who cares!? My play worked! Oh here it is!

I. P. PLAY BOOK
I've been waiting for this day, Alejandro.

I had never seen Izzy this excited in my entire life.
OFFENSE
This is my play binder. I took some of them from my games. I built a few of the others with Eddy. But most of them I made up on my own.
Izzy this is amazing!
86
85

. . . and brought them to my team. We spent the week practicing them. We perfected them.

Here we go. He knows what he's doing. Fake like he's running the old play, and then move to a shotgun. Yes! Great snap.

What's that, Izzy?

Oh sorry—just thinking out loud.

I can't watch.

Packett throws to number 21. He bobs and weaves. He's free! Can he keep going?!

I don't believe it! The first throw of the game and we have a sixty-yard touchdown!
The game started out amazingly. But as the first quarter wound down . . .

. . . my passes started missing.

My team wasn't there for hand offs.

I even threw an interception.
38

That's it!!

Gotta go!

Stop right—oh it's *you*.

You don't understand. It's the plays! I'm—I'm helping.

It took me a moment to realize Izzy had come to the sidelines.

Alejandro, if you want to chat with your family, you can do that from the bench.

I looked at Izzy and at Coach.

I – uh . . .

I wish I hadn't said that. I had a feeling Izzy would have been able to help me more than Coach J. at this point.

Fine!

After the game

Hey Izzy?

Thought you would want to know we lost.

I'm sorry I pushed you away, but Coach didn't really give me a choice.

Anyway, sorry I guess.
Aren't you going to say anything?
I don't get why you care so much. It's not like you're even on the team.
Seriously? You really don't get it.

Last year, after Eddy threw the winning pass, he pointed off the field.

He was pointing at *me*. It was his way of telling me it's my turn to carry on the family football legacy.

We had spent that season making plays together. He wanted me to be team manager and make plays for this season.

But that same jerk who kicked me off the field today wouldn't even talk to me because I was a girl.

You don't know it was because of that.

Yeah I do. Coach J. has some pretty strong ideas of who belongs on that field.

If he didn't, do you think *you* would have been picked for quarterback? Too bad you can't fill your big brother's shoes.

What she said hurt . . . because it felt true.
Hey!
I'm not even trying to be mean. But we both know the only reason you're at quarterback as a tenth grader is because you're Eddy's brother. I just wish I had a chance too.

So, when you asked me for help. It just . . . it meant a lot to me. And tonight . . . what you said really hurt.

Actually, I was pointing at both of you.

Hey lil' bro, lil' sis.

Eddy!

I was okay leaving football knowing you two would keep the Packett name in the game.

Izzy, I'm sorry Coach Vince wouldn't give you a shot.
It's not Coach Vince. Assistant Coach J. is in charge this year.
Oh . . . *him.*

Iz, I'm sorry Coach J. was— no, wait. I'm sorry that *I* was rude to you today. I didn't even give you credit for the plays that were working.

You definitely ranked high on the annoying little brother list this week. But I can forgive you—on one condition.

If the team wants to make it to the playoffs, you'll need my help as manager. And to do that, we'll need a special kind of play—*off* the field.

Now what's so important that Eddy called to ask me to come to practice? You know Coach J. is in charge this season.

Coach, I want you to meet my sister.
Your sister?
Hey Coach. I'm Izzy.
Oh sure! Eddy talked about you last year too. So this is the genius playmaker?
I'm not sure about that, but all of the last game's plays *were* mine—the good and the bad.

You made these?

A lot of them. They were inspired from NFL teams, or video games. And well—

Hold it right there!

I. P. PLAY BOOK

Just what do *you* think you are doing back here?

Hey Coach J.
My sister is chatting with *Head* Coach Vince. Maybe you can give them a minute.
Get out of my way!

You can't seriously think a *girl*–

STOP RIGHT THERE.
No sentence that starts that way ends well. One more word, and I'll walk you off my field, Jeremy.

Whatever!

Apologies Izzy. You were saying . . .

The problem with my plays were that they were based on professional players, not high schoolers. They were too demanding. I needed to adjust my expectations.
So I've made some changes. I . . . I'd like to present them to the team. Maybe . . . as team manager?

I'll do you one better.
13

In no time, it was game night. Game seven. If we wanted a chance at the playoffs, we would need to win the remaining three games.

But with Izzy's plays . . .
Hut– Hut!
. . . and my arm . . .
. . . we had a chance.

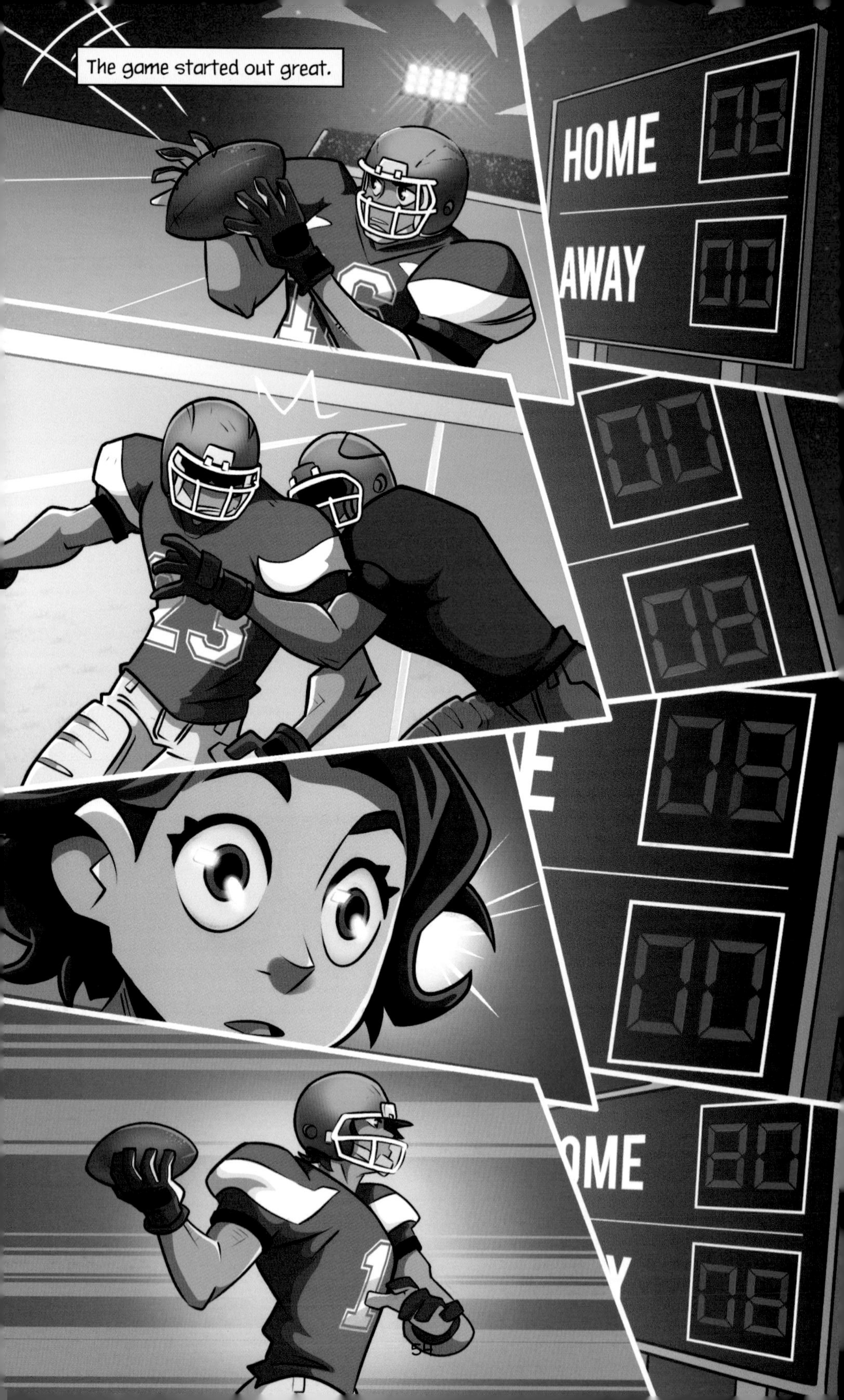

The game started out great.
HOME
AWAY

ME
AWAY
But as the fourth quarter started . . .
ME
AWAY
Everything started spiraling.

Coach Vince called a time out. We had enough time for one more play. We needed a touchdown, but we had more than twenty yards to cover.

I've been pushing the receivers too much. You've made incredible plays but you've been running non-stop.

After the game, Izzy told me how she came up with our final play. Something she would never do in her video game.

Most of the players in Izzy's game are drafted from real teams . . .

But I'm not Eddy. And my brainy big sister knows that. She came up with a play just for me.

. . . the stronger,
faster, brother.
I faked a pass,
and then . . .
. . . I ran faster than
I ever have before.

Once again, Izzy's play started great.
But as I neared the end zone, I could feel the defense closing in. They were coming for the tackle. I braced myself and dove for the end zone.

THUNK!

YES!!

We did it!

Fantastic job, Izzy. With you on the sidelines, we have a real shot at the next two games.
Thanks Coach!

I can't believe that worked!
I can!

I'm so proud
of you two!

VISUAL DISCUSSION QUESTIONS

1. Compare the first interaction between Alejandro and Izzy with the last one in the story. Do you think Alejandro feels the same way at the end as he did in the beginning? Why? What hints does the art give you about how they feel about each other.

2. In graphic novels, the art can often show a character's emotions better than words. How do you think the two coaches are feeling right now?

3. Look at the sequence of panels above. Why do you think the artist chose to show the action this way? If you were drawing this action, would you show it in a different way?

LEARN MORE ABOUT FOOTBALL

Way back in 1869, college players from Princeton and Rutgers College faced off in the first ever football game.

The idea of a huddle in football came from quarterback Paul D. Hubbard. He played from 1892 to 1895. Hubbard was a deaf player, and he was concerned that players on the other team would read his sign language. Then they could adapt to his plays. Gathering his team together in a huddle before each play kept them secret.

Passes in football are measured not just by how far they are thrown, but how far the receiver runs. The longest possible pass in football is 99-yards. That's almost the complete length of the field. Only 13 quarterbacks have thrown this pass. The first was Frank Filchock in 1939. He threw it 9-yards to Andy Farkas. Farkas then ran the remaining 90-yards to score.

Starting in the mid 1990's, the National Football League (NFL) began hosting a Madden Video Game tournament alongside the Super Bowl. When it started, the participants were celebrities and NFL players. The Madden Bowl has kept going, but now, the competitors are the best Madden players in esports from around the world.

The highest scoring NFL game was in 1966. Washington's team, now called the Commanders, won 72 to 41 against the New York Giants. The game had a grand total of 113 points scored.

FOOTBALL TERMS YOU SHOULD KNOW

downfield—the direction on the field that the offense is moving toward

huddle—a gathering of football players on a team before a play

interception—when a defensive player catches a pass thrown by the offensive quarterback

offensive line—a group of a football team's largest players who protect the quarterback and create openings for other players to move the ball down the field

playbook—a collection of a team's football plays gathered into a binder or notebook

playoffs—a series of games played after the regular season to determine a champion

quarterback—the player who runs the offense; the quarterback can run, hand off the ball, or make a pass

receiver—an offensive player who catches passes and runs the ball downfield

sidelines—the area outside of the field where coaches and standby players watch the game

touchdown—a six-point score made by moving the ball over an opposing team's goal line

GLOSSARY

captain (CAP-tuhn)—the leader of a sports team

decisive (dee-SIGH-siv)—able to make quick, firm decisions

genius (JEE-nyuhss)—someone who is exceptionally smart

imaginary (i-MAJ-uh-ner-ee)—existing in the mind and not in the real world

legacy (LEG-uh-see)—qualities and actions that one is remembered for; something that is passed into the future

manager (MAN-uh-jur)—a person in charge of a group

option (OP-shuhn)—multiple choices a person can make in the moment

record (REK-urd)—the number of wins and losses

strategy (STRAT-uh-jee)—a plan for winning a game, race, or contest of some sort

ABOUT THE AUTHOR

Daniel Mauleón grew up playing video games more than sports and identifies with the basement dwelling Izzy. However, in high school during a game of pick-up football on Halloween, he scored a touchdown in a suit and tie.

Daniel graduated from Hamline University with a Masters in Fine Arts for Writing for Children and Young Adults in 2017 and has written a variety of books and graphic novels since. He lives with his wife, and two cats, in Minnesota.

ABOUT THE ARTISTS

Berenice Muñiz is a graphic designer and illustrator from Monterrey, Mexico. She has done work for publicity agencies, art exhibitions, and even created her own webcomic. These days, Berenice is devoted to illustrating comics as part of the Graphikslava crew.

Amaury Maldonado is a multimedia and animation engineer born in Monterrey, Nuevo León, México. A freelance artist and colorist, he is currently studying to specialize in modeling and 3D rigging. He is a fan of good stories and videogames. He likes creating characters and developing fantasy environments.

READ THEM ALL!

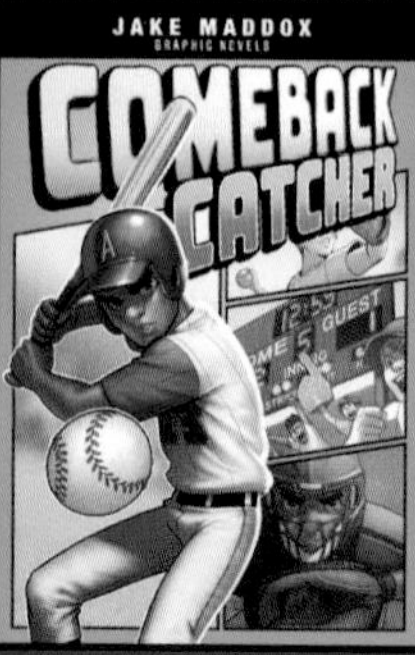

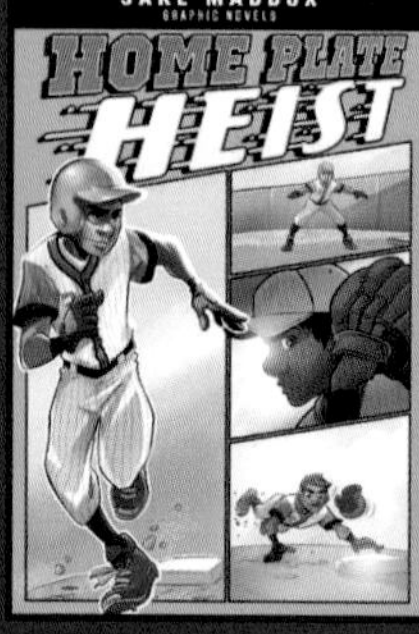

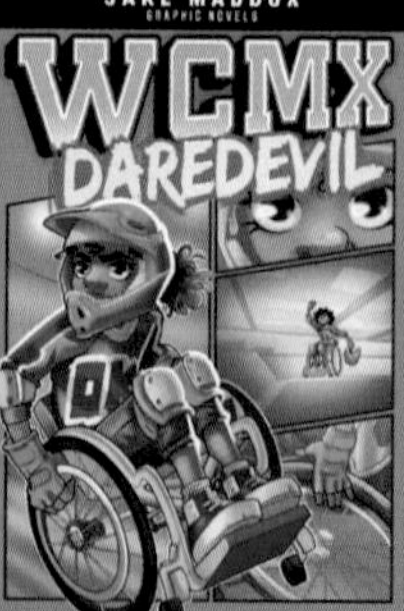